CHILDREN'S STORYTIME TREASURY

Hans Andersen's Fairytales

A PARRAGON BOOK

PUBLISHED BY PARRAGON BOOK SERVICE LTD.
UNITS 13-17, AVONBRIDGE TRADING ESTATE, ATLANTIC ROAD,
AVONMOUTH, BRISTOL BS11 9QD

PRODUCED BY THE TEMPLAR COMPANY PLC,
PIPPBROOK MILL, LONDON ROAD, DORKING, SURREY RH4 1JE

DESIGNED BY MARK KINGSLEY-MONKS

PRINTED AND BOUND IN SPAIN

ISBN 0-75252-037-7

CHILDREN'S STORYTIME TREASURY

Hans Andersen's Fairytales

· PARRAGON ·

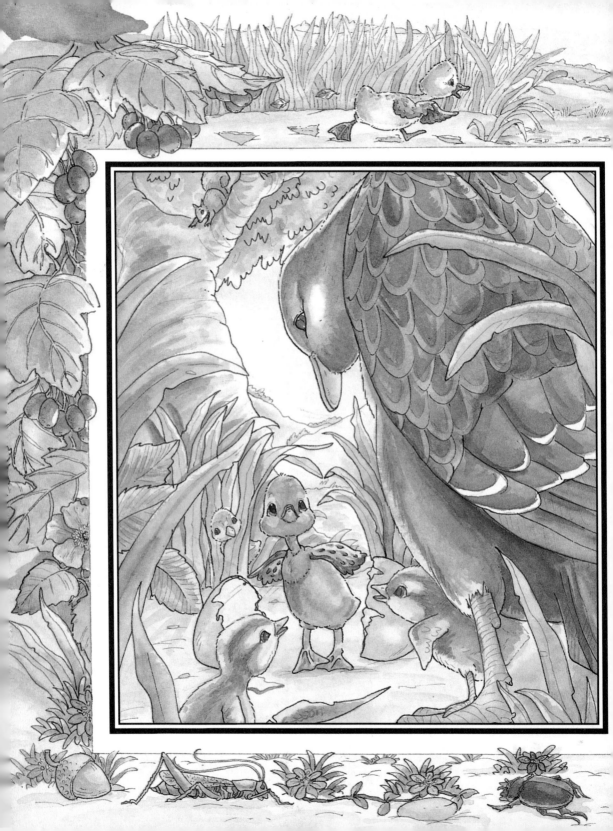

The Ugly Duckling

Illustrated by Andrew Geeson

There was once a little mother duck. She had six eggs in her nest and there she sat day after day in the summer sun patiently waiting for them to hatch. Five of the eggs were small and white but the sixth egg was large and brown. The little duck often wondered why that egg was so different.

One morning she heard a crack, then another, then another. Her chicks were ready! One by one they tumbled from their shells and soon five little chicks were gathered under the wings of their proud mother. But the large brown egg had not hatched.

"What can be keeping my last little chick?" thought the mother duck to herself and she settled herself on top of the egg to keep it warm.

At last she felt the egg moving and out scrambled a chick. But this chick was nothing like her other babies. He was covered in dull brown fluff and had a long scrawny neck. He wasn't nearly as pretty as his brothers and sisters. But the mother duck loved him just the same and took care to protect him from the other farmyard animals who often teased him.

"Did you ever see anything quite as ugly as that gawky looking creature?" squawked a large brown duck to his friend, the white hen.

"Go away!" clucked the hen. "We don't want you in our farmyard," and she pecked at the poor little duckling with her sharp beak.

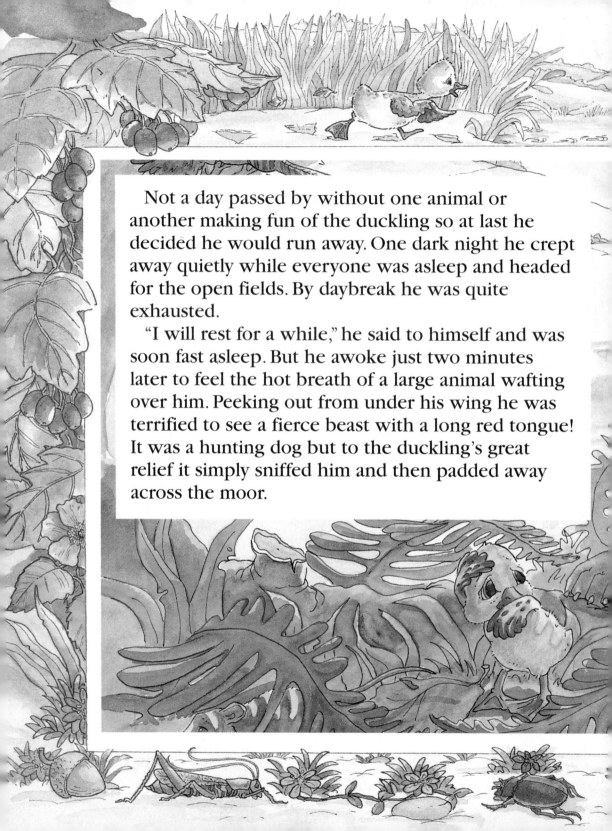

Not a day passed by without one animal or another making fun of the duckling so at last he decided he would run away. One dark night he crept away quietly while everyone was asleep and headed for the open fields. By daybreak he was quite exhausted.

"I will rest for a while," he said to himself and was soon fast asleep. But he awoke just two minutes later to feel the hot breath of a large animal wafting over him. Peeking out from under his wing he was terrified to see a fierce beast with a long red tongue! It was a hunting dog but to the duckling's great relief it simply sniffed him and then padded away across the moor.

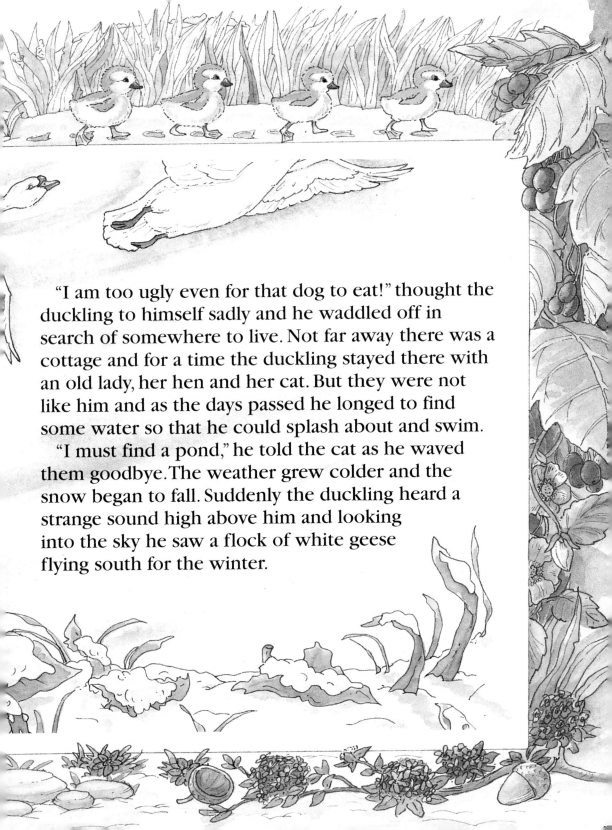

"I am too ugly even for that dog to eat!" thought the duckling to himself sadly and he waddled off in search of somewhere to live. Not far away there was a cottage and for a time the duckling stayed there with an old lady, her hen and her cat. But they were not like him and as the days passed he longed to find some water so that he could splash about and swim.

"I must find a pond," he told the cat as he waved them goodbye. The weather grew colder and the snow began to fall. Suddenly the duckling heard a strange sound high above him and looking into the sky he saw a flock of white geese flying south for the winter.

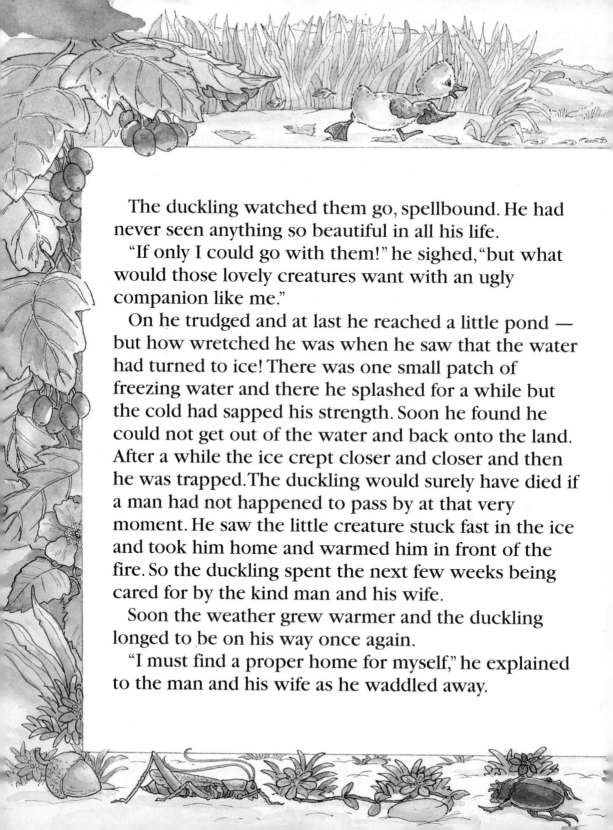

The duckling watched them go, spellbound. He had never seen anything so beautiful in all his life.

"If only I could go with them!" he sighed, "but what would those lovely creatures want with an ugly companion like me."

On he trudged and at last he reached a little pond — but how wretched he was when he saw that the water had turned to ice! There was one small patch of freezing water and there he splashed for a while but the cold had sapped his strength. Soon he found he could not get out of the water and back onto the land. After a while the ice crept closer and closer and then he was trapped. The duckling would surely have died if a man had not happened to pass by at that very moment. He saw the little creature stuck fast in the ice and took him home and warmed him in front of the fire. So the duckling spent the next few weeks being cared for by the kind man and his wife.

Soon the weather grew warmer and the duckling longed to be on his way once again.

"I must find a proper home for myself," he explained to the man and his wife as he waddled away.

The air grew softer, the birds sang and the flowers bloomed in the meadows once again. The duckling felt stronger and he noticed that his feet and his body had grown much bigger and seemed to be changing colour. He felt happy and excited and, stretching out his wings, he beat them up and down for fun. Just imagine his astonishment when he suddenly found himself leaving the ground and flying through the air! What a glorious feeling it was to be soaring on high.

"Here in the sky I am free!" he said to himself happily. All at once he saw something exciting far below him. As he swooped down to get a better look he recognised the snow white birds who had flown over him on their way south. Now they had returned and were splashing in the pond. The duckling landed on the water and slowly swam towards them.

"I know I am ugly," he said shyly, "but please let me stay with you and be your friend."

"Why, you are not ugly!" laughed the birds. "You have become a beautiful swan just like us," and as the duckling bowed his head to look in the water he saw that it was indeed true!

The Steadfast Tin Soldier

Illustrated by Helen Smith

There was once a Tin Soldier. He was exactly the same as his twenty-four brothers, but for one thing. He had only one leg! When he was made, the tin ran out just as it was about to be poured into his second leg, but he could still stand straight and tall.

He lived in the nursery with all the other toys but his favourite by far was a pretty little lady who stood on one toe and pointed her other foot high in the air. Why, it was almost as if she had only one leg, just like him! She was made all of paper and held her arms gracefully above her head, for she was a Dancer.

The Steadfast Tin Soldier loved to watch her and stood perfectly still for hour after hour gazing at her lovely face and wishing he could speak to her.

"But what is the use of trying to win her love?" he sighed. "She lives in a grand castle and I have to share a wooden box with my twenty-four brothers."

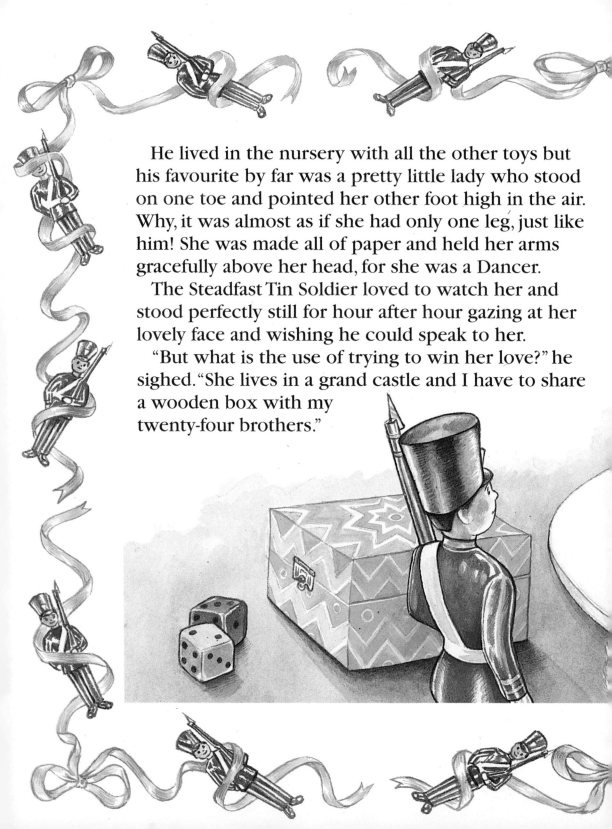

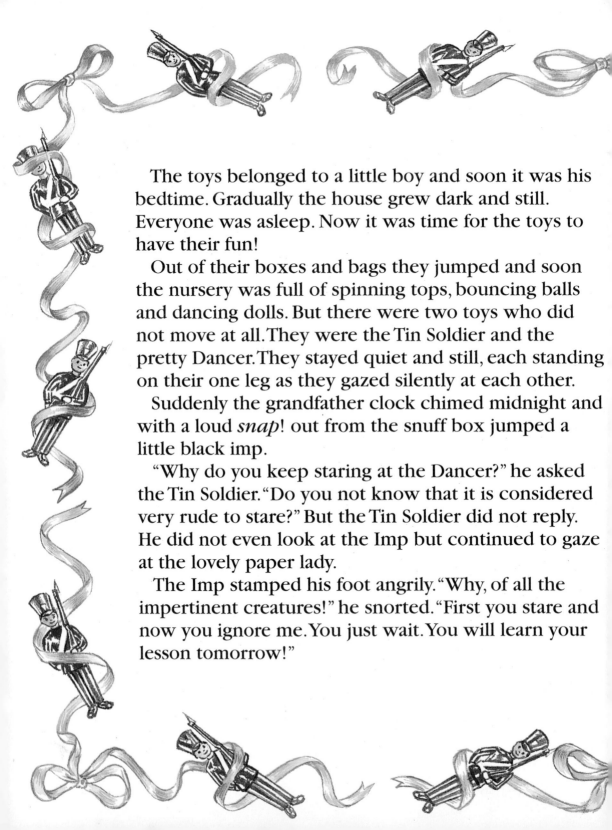

The toys belonged to a little boy and soon it was his bedtime. Gradually the house grew dark and still. Everyone was asleep. Now it was time for the toys to have their fun!

Out of their boxes and bags they jumped and soon the nursery was full of spinning tops, bouncing balls and dancing dolls. But there were two toys who did not move at all. They were the Tin Soldier and the pretty Dancer. They stayed quiet and still, each standing on their one leg as they gazed silently at each other.

Suddenly the grandfather clock chimed midnight and with a loud *snap*! out from the snuff box jumped a little black imp.

"Why do you keep staring at the Dancer?" he asked the Tin Soldier. "Do you not know that it is considered very rude to stare?" But the Tin Soldier did not reply. He did not even look at the Imp but continued to gaze at the lovely paper lady.

The Imp stamped his foot angrily. "Why, of all the impertinent creatures!" he snorted. "First you stare and now you ignore me. You just wait. You will learn your lesson tomorrow!"

The next day the little boy played with the one-legged Tin Soldier and when he went for his tea he left him standing on the windowsill. Now whether it was the wind or whether it was the little black imp up to his tricks, who can say, but all of a sudden the window flew open and the Soldier was blown outside!

Down he tumbled and with a bump landed upside down between two paving stones. There he stayed, firmly wedged, while the little boy searched high and low. If only the soldier had called out he would have been found in an instant but he was proud and felt that no soldier should have to call for help. The little boy returned indoors and soon it began to rain. The raindrops fell faster and faster and before long there was a real downpour.

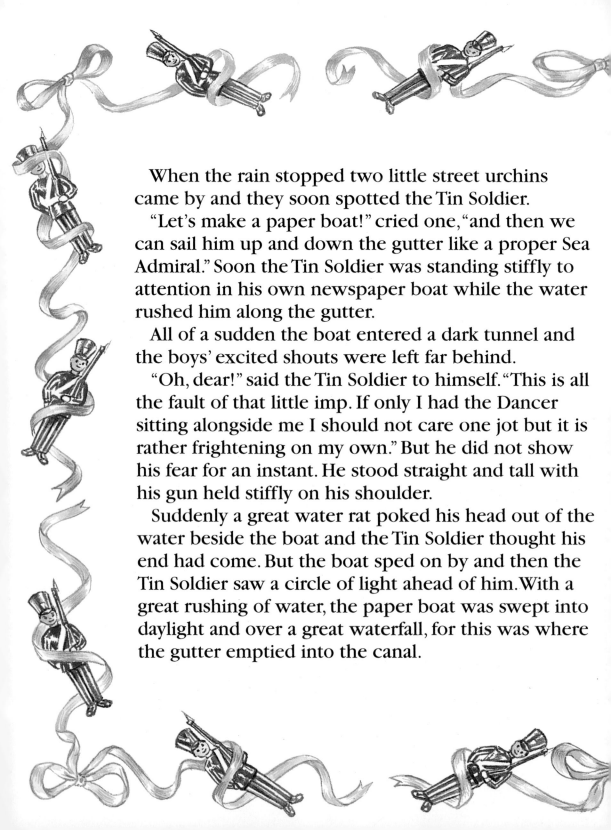

When the rain stopped two little street urchins came by and they soon spotted the Tin Soldier.

"Let's make a paper boat!" cried one, "and then we can sail him up and down the gutter like a proper Sea Admiral." Soon the Tin Soldier was standing stiffly to attention in his own newspaper boat while the water rushed him along the gutter.

All of a sudden the boat entered a dark tunnel and the boys' excited shouts were left far behind.

"Oh, dear!" said the Tin Soldier to himself. "This is all the fault of that little imp. If only I had the Dancer sitting alongside me I should not care one jot but it is rather frightening on my own." But he did not show his fear for an instant. He stood straight and tall with his gun held stiffly on his shoulder.

Suddenly a great water rat poked his head out of the water beside the boat and the Tin Soldier thought his end had come. But the boat sped on by and then the Tin Soldier saw a circle of light ahead of him. With a great rushing of water, the paper boat was swept into daylight and over a great waterfall, for this was where the gutter emptied into the canal.

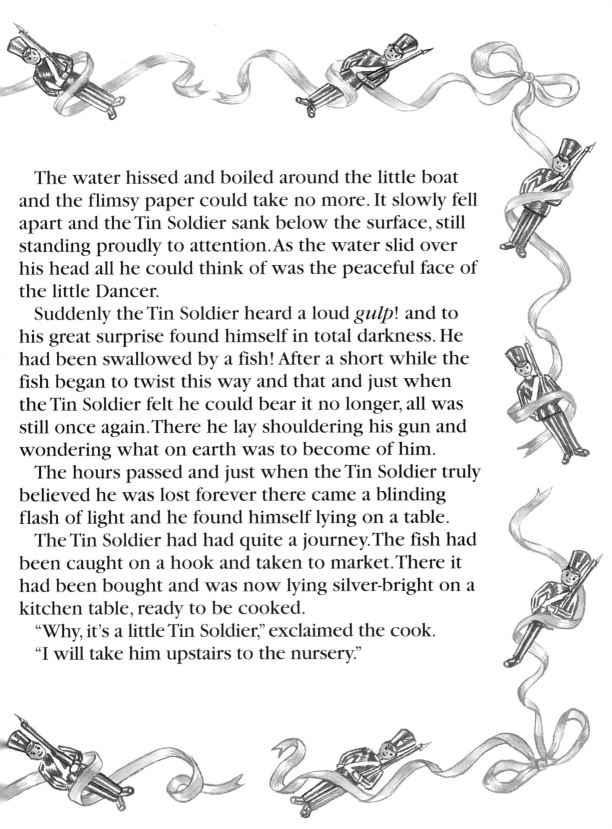

The water hissed and boiled around the little boat and the flimsy paper could take no more. It slowly fell apart and the Tin Soldier sank below the surface, still standing proudly to attention. As the water slid over his head all he could think of was the peaceful face of the little Dancer.

Suddenly the Tin Soldier heard a loud *gulp*! and to his great surprise found himself in total darkness. He had been swallowed by a fish! After a short while the fish began to twist this way and that and just when the Tin Soldier felt he could bear it no longer, all was still once again. There he lay shouldering his gun and wondering what on earth was to become of him.

The hours passed and just when the Tin Soldier truly believed he was lost forever there came a blinding flash of light and he found himself lying on a table.

The Tin Soldier had had quite a journey. The fish had been caught on a hook and taken to market. There it had been bought and was now lying silver-bright on a kitchen table, ready to be cooked.

"Why, it's a little Tin Soldier," exclaimed the cook.

"I will take him upstairs to the nursery."

So it was that the little Tin Soldier found himself standing on a table and looking into the face of a little boy. Well, what strange things do happen in this world! He was in his old nursery and there was the pretty Dancer still standing on one toe the same as she always did.

But the boy was not pleased to see the Tin Soldier. Maybe it was because he looked so shabby, or maybe the little black imp had something to do with it, but he snatched up the Tin Soldier and threw him in the fire!

There he stood, as brave as could be, and the flames flickered around him. He looked straight at the paper lady and she looked right back at him.

Suddenly the door opened and a draught picked the paper lady off the table and carried her through the air. Straight towards the fire she floated and there she landed right in the arms of the Tin Soldier. As her arms brushed his cheek she burst into flames and was gone. Then the Tin Soldier finally melted.

The next morning when the maid swept out the fire she found a cinder of black paper and a small lump of tin in the shape of a heart — all that was left of the Dancer and her Steadfast Tin Soldier.

The Little Mermaid
Illustrated by Roger Langton

F ar, far out to sea, where the water was deep and blue, the Mer People swam in their underwater grottoes. The Mer King had a fine palace made all of coral and there he lived with his six daughters. They loved their life under the sea but when the youngest daughter caught her first glimpse of the upper world, she thought it was the most wonderful place she had ever seen.

One evening the little Mermaid watched spellbound as a fine ship came sailing close by. She was near enough to see a young man in one of the cabins. He was a Prince and the Mermaid thought him the most handsome man in the world. Suddenly there was a loud clap of thunder and black clouds rolled across the sky. The wind whipped the waves as high as hills and, to the Mermaid's great terror, the great ship was struck by lightning and split right in two. The sea was full of men, all shrieking and wailing and there, clinging to a spar, was the handsome Prince. She took hold of his arm and, swimming strongly, towed him to land.

As he lay upon the beach a young girl found him and called for help. The Prince opened his eyes and believed that she was the one who had saved him. Only the little Mermaid, hiding behind a rock, knew the real truth. Before the Prince could ask who she was, the young girl ran off and so the Prince's rescue remained a mystery. But the little Mermaid could not forget him and every evening she swam to the surface of the sea and gazed at the palace where he lived.

"Come home with us," said her sisters, but the Mermaid longed to catch another glimpse of the Prince.

"You cannot share his life," they scolded. "You have a silver tail and will never be able to walk on dry land. You must forget him." But the Mermaid could think of nothing else. She would not be happy until she was rid of her tail and able to visit the upper world.

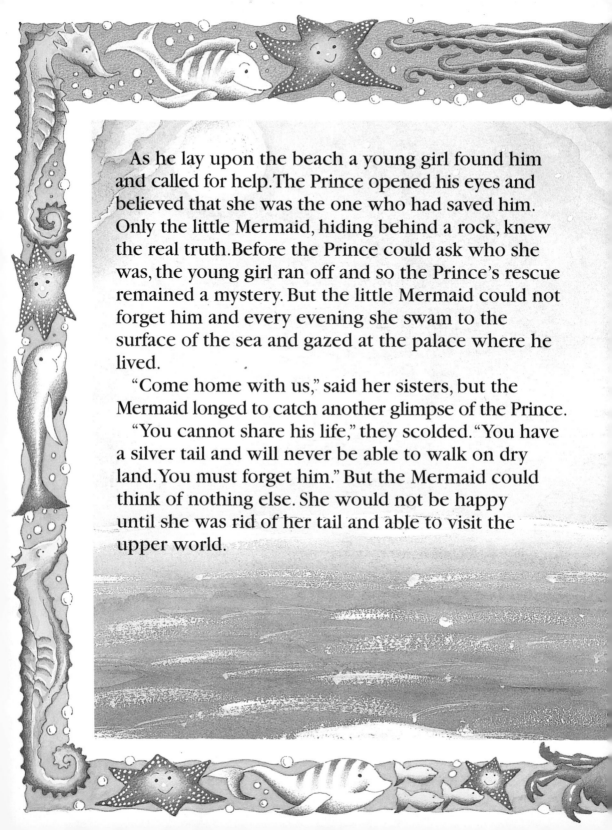

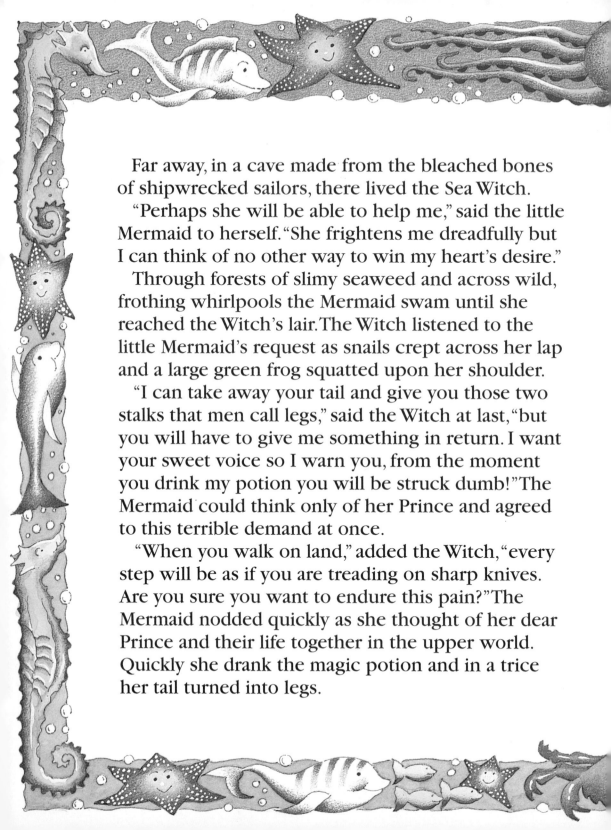

Far away, in a cave made from the bleached bones of shipwrecked sailors, there lived the Sea Witch.

"Perhaps she will be able to help me," said the little Mermaid to herself. "She frightens me dreadfully but I can think of no other way to win my heart's desire."

Through forests of slimy seaweed and across wild, frothing whirlpools the Mermaid swam until she reached the Witch's lair. The Witch listened to the little Mermaid's request as snails crept across her lap and a large green frog squatted upon her shoulder.

"I can take away your tail and give you those two stalks that men call legs," said the Witch at last, "but you will have to give me something in return. I want your sweet voice so I warn you, from the moment you drink my potion you will be struck dumb!" The Mermaid could think only of her Prince and agreed to this terrible demand at once.

"When you walk on land," added the Witch, "every step will be as if you are treading on sharp knives. Are you sure you want to endure this pain?" The Mermaid nodded quickly as she thought of her dear Prince and their life together in the upper world. Quickly she drank the magic potion and in a trice her tail turned into legs.

She found herself lying upon the marble steps beside the Prince's palace and when she was discovered by the Queen's maids she was dressed and brought before the royal family. They were all captivated by her beauty and sweet nature but when they asked who she was, the Mermaid could not say a word.

Gentle music filled the air and the Mermaid could not help but dance. She moved gracefully across the floor, spinning and twirling, but every step was agony and soon her eyes were filled with tears. The Prince held her in his arms and felt great pity and tenderness for the little girl but it was clear to the Mermaid that he did not share the same love that she had for him. As the weeks passed the Prince showed nothing but kindness to the Mermaid, but she longed for a love to equal her own.

Soon the time came for the Prince to take a bride and the King and Queen announced that he would marry the daughter of a neighbouring king. As the Prince was introduced to the Princess the little Mermaid thought her heart would break for the girl was the same girl who had knelt by the Prince's side on the beach so long ago.

"You are the one who saved me!" cried the Prince, but the silent Mermaid could not explain the truth.

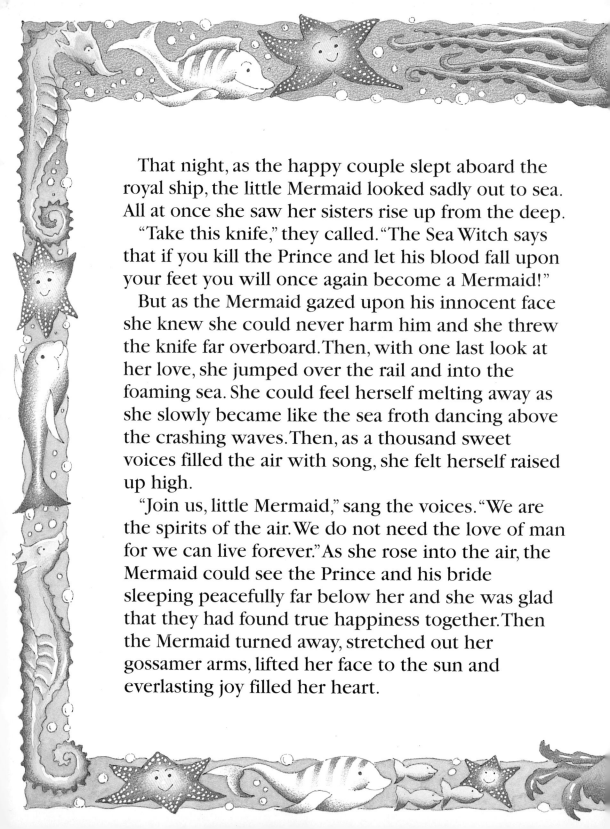

That night, as the happy couple slept aboard the royal ship, the little Mermaid looked sadly out to sea. All at once she saw her sisters rise up from the deep.

"Take this knife," they called. "The Sea Witch says that if you kill the Prince and let his blood fall upon your feet you will once again become a Mermaid!"

But as the Mermaid gazed upon his innocent face she knew she could never harm him and she threw the knife far overboard. Then, with one last look at her love, she jumped over the rail and into the foaming sea. She could feel herself melting away as she slowly became like the sea froth dancing above the crashing waves. Then, as a thousand sweet voices filled the air with song, she felt herself raised up high.

"Join us, little Mermaid," sang the voices. "We are the spirits of the air. We do not need the love of man for we can live forever." As she rose into the air, the Mermaid could see the Prince and his bride sleeping peacefully far below her and she was glad that they had found true happiness together. Then the Mermaid turned away, stretched out her gossamer arms, lifted her face to the sun and everlasting joy filled her heart.

The Little Matchgirl

Illustrated by Annabel Spenceley

It was New Year's Eve and the little matchgirl clutched her bundle of matches in a hand that was numb with cold. All day long she sat huddled on the pavement but not a single person stopped to buy and she had not earned so much as a single penny. She was very hungry but knew she could not return to her poor home until every match had been sold. She shivered as the icy wind whipped around her bare feet and the snow fell in flurries about her head.

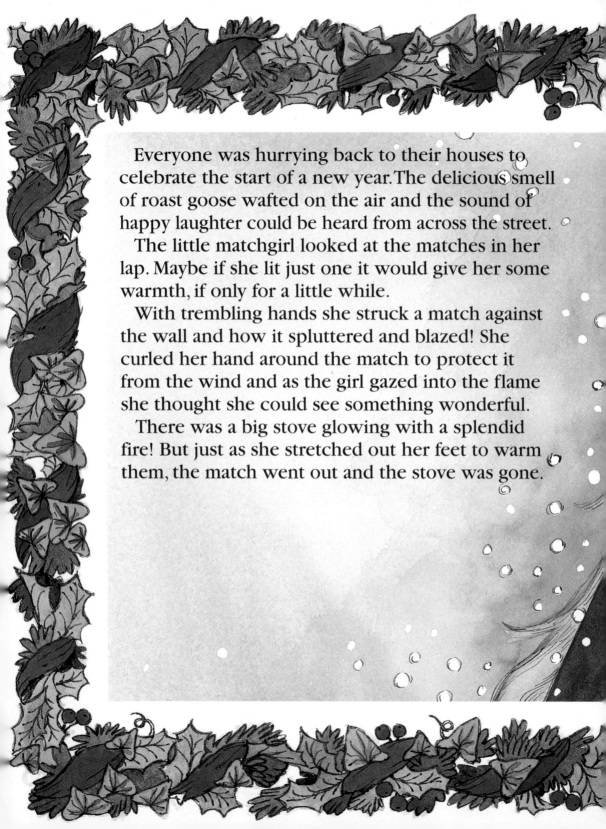

Everyone was hurrying back to their houses to celebrate the start of a new year. The delicious smell of roast goose wafted on the air and the sound of happy laughter could be heard from across the street.

The little matchgirl looked at the matches in her lap. Maybe if she lit just one it would give her some warmth, if only for a little while.

With trembling hands she struck a match against the wall and how it spluttered and blazed! She curled her hand around the match to protect it from the wind and as the girl gazed into the flame she thought she could see something wonderful.

There was a big stove glowing with a splendid fire! But just as she stretched out her feet to warm them, the match went out and the stove was gone.

How desperate the little girl felt when she looked at
the burnt-out match in her hand. She simply *had* to feel
that comforting warmth again. Slowly she took another
match and struck it once more upon the wall. It blazed
up and where the light fell upon the bricks they
became transparent and the little matchgirl was sure
she could see right through and into the room on the
other side.

There was a table all laid for dinner and in the middle
sat a large roast goose, glistening and golden. The
matchgirl could smell the savoury meat and her eyes
shone as she looked at it hungrily. It seemed to come
closer and closer—then the light went out and there
was nothing to be seen but a cold black wall.

"Just one more match!" said the little girl to herself
and this time the flame showed her a beautiful green
Christmas tree covered with glowing candles. But in no
time at all the match had burnt down and the tree
disappeared. But the candles had not gone. Their bright
little lights rose higher and higher until the matchgirl
could see that they were twinkling stars.

Suddenly one of them fell across the sky.

"Someone is dying," thought the little girl. "My dear grandmother used to tell me that when a star falls, a soul is going up to God." She struck another match against the wall and this time she gave a cry of surprise for there was her grandmother in a warm circle of flame and she looked so very happy.

"Grandmother!" cried the little girl. "Oh, do take me with you. You will vanish when the match goes out, just like the warm stove, the delicious goose and the beautiful tree. Please do not leave me here!"

Then the little matchgirl struck match after match against the wall because she wanted so much to keep her grandmother near her. The light of the matches made the night as bright as day and grandmother had never looked so beautiful. Gently she gathered the little girl in her arms and together they soared in a halo of light and joy far above the earth where there was no more cold, no hunger and no pain, for now they were with God.

And as the cold morning light crept over the horizon it found the little girl huddled against the wall. She was dead but her pale face shone with a wonderful smile.

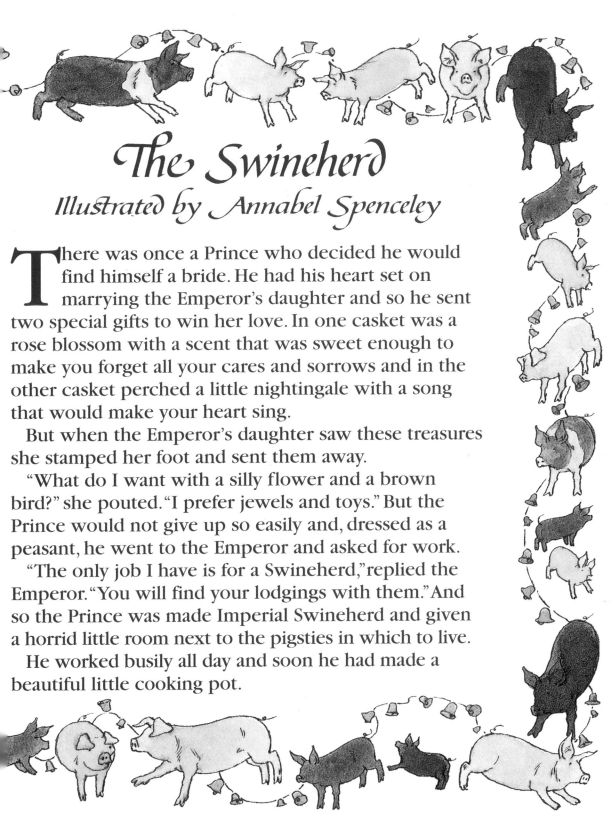

The Swineherd

Illustrated by Annabel Spenceley

There was once a Prince who decided he would find himself a bride. He had his heart set on marrying the Emperor's daughter and so he sent two special gifts to win her love. In one casket was a rose blossom with a scent that was sweet enough to make you forget all your cares and sorrows and in the other casket perched a little nightingale with a song that would make your heart sing.

But when the Emperor's daughter saw these treasures she stamped her foot and sent them away.

"What do I want with a silly flower and a brown bird?" she pouted. "I prefer jewels and toys." But the Prince would not give up so easily and, dressed as a peasant, he went to the Emperor and asked for work.

"The only job I have is for a Swineherd," replied the Emperor. "You will find your lodgings with them." And so the Prince was made Imperial Swineherd and given a horrid little room next to the pigsties in which to live.

He worked busily all day and soon he had made a beautiful little cooking pot.

If you held your finger in the steam you could smell what everyone in the palace was cooking for their dinner, from the Lord Chancellor's roast beef right down to the scullery maid's thin gruel.

The next day the Princess came by and when she heard the magical, musical pot she sent her lady-in-waiting to ask what it would cost. What a shock!

"The Swineherd is asking for ten kisses from Your Royal Highness!" the maid gasped. The Princess was outraged by this impertinence but the more she thought of the pot, the more she wanted it and so at last she gave in and the Swineherd took his ten kisses.

The magic pot was a great success but the Swineherd did not stop there. He set to and made a singing rattle and when he swung it around his head it played the jolliest of waltzes and polkas. When the Princess heard the rattle she was determined to make it hers. But how dismayed she was to hear that this time the naughty Swineherd wanted a hundred kisses!

"It is a terrible thing for the Emperor's daughter to be seen kissing a Swineherd," said the Princess, "but I must encourage a true artist and so I will do as he asks."

From his window the Emperor could see a little crowd clustered in front of the pigsties.

"What are the ladies-in-waiting up to now?" he said. "I will tiptoe up behind them and find out." Softly, softly he crept into the pig yard and there he saw his beloved daughter in the arms of the filthy swineherd!

"What is the meaning of this?" he thundered as he fell about the Swineherd with his slipper. "You are both banished from the palace!" and the poor Princess and the disguised Prince were locked outside the gates.

"Now what is to become of me?" wailed the forlorn Princess. "If only I had married that Prince while I had the chance." Then the Swineherd went behind a tree and changed out of his dirty clothes. When he next stepped before her he was dressed as a fine Prince and the Princess blushed and curtsied prettily in front of him.

But the Prince was not impressed. "You did not appreciate my gifts of the rose and the nightingale," he said sternly, "but you would kiss the Swineherd for a silly musical pot! You have made your bed and now you must lie in it!"

And so the Prince returned to his own kingdom and left the Princess with only a pot and a rattle for company.

OTHER TITLES IN THIS SERIES INCLUDE:

AESOP'S FABLES

GRIMM'S FAIRYTALES

JUST-SO STORIES

NURSERY TALES

TALES FROM THE ARABIAN NIGHTS

TALES OF BRER RABBIT

WIND IN THE WILLOWS